Fire Light Fire Bright

a Firehawks romance story

by

M. L. Buchman

Buchman Bookworks

Other works by M.L. Buchman

The Night Stalkers

The Night Is Mine
I Own the Dawn
Daniel's Christmas
Wait Until Dark
Frank's Independence Day
Peter's Christmas
Take Over at Midnight
Light Up the Night

Firehawks

Pure Heat
Wildfire at Dawn
Full Blaze

Angelo's Hearth

Where Dreams are Born
Where Dreams Reside
Maria's Christmas Table
Where Dreams Unfold
Where Dreams Are Written

Dieties Anonymous

Cookbook from Hell: Reheated
Saviors 101

Thrillers

Swap Out!

One Chef!
Two Chef!

SF/F Titles
Nara
Monk's Maze

1

"Hi, I'm Candace Cantrell. First Rule: anyome calls me Candy, who isn't my dad," she hooked a thumb at Fire Chief Carl Cantrell standing at-ease beside her, "is gonna get my boot up their ass. We clear on that?"

A rolling mumble of "Yes, ma'am." "Clear." and "Got it, Candace." rippled back to her from the recruits. Some answered almost as softly as the breeze working its way up through the tall pines. Others trumpeting it out as if to get her notice. A few offered simple nods.

She surveyed the line of recruits slowly. Way too early to make any judgments, but it was tempting. Day One, Minute One, and she could already guess five of the forty applicants weren't going to make it into the twenty slots she had open.

The one thing they all, including her dad, needed to see right up front was their team leader's complete confidence. Candace had been fighting wildfires for the U.S. Forest Service hotshot teams for a decade. She'd worked her way up to foreman twice, and had been gunning for a shot at superintendent of a whole twenty-person crew when her dad had called.

"We've got permission to form up an IHC in the heart of the Okanagan-Wenatchee National Forest," he never was long on greetings over the phone.

Her mouth had watered. A brand new Interagency Hotshot Crew didn't happen all that often.

"I talked to the other captains and we want you to form it up."

Now her throat had gone dry and she had to fight not to let it squeak.

"Me?"

"You aren't gonna let me down now, Candy Girl?"

"You shittin' me?" Not a chance.

Then he'd hit her with that big belly laugh of his.

"Knew you'd like the idea."

And simple as that, she'd been out of the San Juan IHC at the end of the Colorado fire season and back home in the Cascade Mountains of Washington State. She'd grown up in the resort town of Leavenworth—two thousand people and a ka-jillion tourists. The city fathers had transformed the failing timber town into a Bavarian wonderland back in the sixties. But that didn't stop the millions of acres of the National Forest and the rugged sagebrush-steppe ecosystem further east in central Washington from torching off every summer.

The very first thing she'd done, before she'd even left the San Juan IHC, was to call in a pair of ringers as her two foremen. Jess was short, feisty, and could walk up forested mountains all day with heavy gear without slowing down a bit. Patsy was tall, quiet, and tough. Candace had them stand in with the crews for the first days because she wanted their eyes out there as well.

"Second, see that road?" she asked the recruits and pointed to the foot of National Forest Road 6500. She'd had their first meet-up be here rather than at the fire hall in town. A gaggle of vehicles were pulled off the dirt of Little Wenatchee River Road. Beater pickups dominated, but there were a couple of hammered Civics, a pair of muscle cars, and a gorgeous Harley Davidson that she considered stealing it was so sweet.

The recruits all looked over their shoulders at the one lane of dirt.

"We're going for a walk up that road. We leave in sixty seconds."

Like a herd of sheep, they all swung their heads to look at her.

"Fifty-five seconds, and this ain't gonna be a Sunday stroll."

You could tell the number of seasons they'd fought fire just by their reactions.

Five or more? They already wore their boots. Daypacks with water and energy bars were kept on their shoulders during her intro. And despite it being Day One of the ten-day shakedown, all had some tools: fold-up shovel and a heavy knife strapped to their leg at a minimum. Only she, Jess, and Patsy had Pulaski wildland fire axes tied to their gear, but all the veterans knew the drill.

Three to four seasons? Groans and eyerolls. Packs were on the ground beside them. No tools, but they knew what was coming now that she'd told them—ten kilometers, at least, and not one meter of it flat.

One to two seasons? Had the right boots on, but no packs. They were racing back to their vehicles to see what equipment they could assemble.

Rookies? Tennis shoes, ball caps, no gear, blank stares.

"Forty-five seconds, rooks. Boots and water. If you're not on the trail in fifty seconds, you're off the crew." That got their asses moving.

There was one man on the whole crew she couldn't pigeonhole, the big guy who'd climbed off the Harley. His pack and the fold-up shovel strapped to it were so new they sparkled. But his boots and the massive hunting knife on his thigh both showed very heavy use.

A glance at her dad's assessing gaze confirmed it. Something was odd about the Harley man and his easy grin. Not rugged handsome, but still very nice to look at. Powerful shoulders, slim waist. Not an athlete's build, but rather someone who really used his body. His worn jeans revealed that he already had the powerful legs that every hotshot would develop from endless miles of chasing fire over these mountains and steppes for the next six months. It was like he was a Hollywood movie: some parts of him were so very right, but a lot of the details were dead wrong.

2

Luke Rawlings looked at the team super-intendent. Couldn't help himself, 'cause damn she was a treat to look at. Her white-blond hair was short and sassy, her body was seriously fit, but curved like a sweet-Candy dream girl. Her no-nonsense attitude just cracked him up; he could hear that natural state of command that you only learned the hard way, by doing it. Not something he'd ever expected to find in a hot civilian babe.

When he'd mustered out, SEAL Lieutenant Commander Altman had suggested he try firefighting. Altman was a smart dude, so Luke had followed his suggestion. He'd kicked around with a big city fire department doing ride-alongs for a while. Chicago Fire were all super guys and they kept trying to sign him aboard, but tramping pavement and cement, doing fire inspections for date tags on commercial fire extinguishers…he'd rather be back in the African jungle. If his nerves would let him, which he so wasn't going to think about now.

He still wasn't sure how he'd heard about the hotshot crews, but walking into a wildfire—he just liked the way it sounded.

And looking at "Not Candy" Cantrell, he was damn glad he'd followed his whim and ridden his Harley west. "Not Candy." What did that make her? Cake, or main course?

She moved to the head of the dirt forest road where it left the pavement. The old hands had already moved onto the track, but they waited once there. So, hotshot teams moved as a unit. Good. That was familiar.

He dropped into line to watch. Candace had already picked out at least two of her team, he could see the surreptitious communication between the three of them; all three with worn fireaxes, despite it being just a training walk.

Number One tool of their trade. Got it.

So, her recruit assessment was underway from the inside as well. The two insiders were watching the rookies, but the superintendent also had her eye tracking him.

Didn't require his kind of training to catch the glance between father and daughter as they assessed him. Let them wonder. There were some things he'd rather not talk about. He was just gonna play Mr. Average Joe Firefighter Hopeful and see how it rolled.

3

Day Five and Candace was halfway through the selection process. She'd been right on four out of the five who'd been gone on Day One; one had made it to Day Two. She'd lost five more since then. She was down from forty to thirty on her way to the final twenty to be accepted into the crew.

She knew crew bosses who did it solely with physical testing: massive hikes, hard calisthenics, and so on. She preferred to incorporate as much training as possible.

Here's what the real world will be like, kids. You up for it?

Yesterday she had them clearing a line. When a fire was working its way through the forest duff and detritus, it was up to a hotshot team to scrape and clear a wide swath down to mineral soil, and to do it in lines often a mile or more long. Upslope and down.

Hotshots might be the elite ground crew, barely a step down from the smoke-jumpers, but they spent a lot of time grubbing dirt lines. Sixteen hours she'd kept them at it, sunup to well past sundown, finishing by headlamp, then sacking out right where they were. On a big fire, they'd be going twenty-four to thirty-six hours at a time and she wanted to give them a taste of that. They all wore field packs now and either a Pulaski axe or a McLeod rake. Unlike most field duty during the season, her dad's townie crew did roll in with a wildfire engine loaded up for each meal; so at least they ate well.

Today, she pulled Jess and Patsy out of the crowd and introduced them around the deep woods camp as her two foremen. She'd left them in the team long enough that their exceptional skills and experience had become standout obvious, so there were no hard feelings about having spies in their midst. At least none that she could spot.

Luke Rawlings had offered her one of his enigmatic smiles that seemed to say, *About time.* As if he'd known about them since the first day.

She was half tempted to boot the man, just because the puzzle of him was so damned distracting. Candace needed the team to stay focused and this man was a complete aberration. But the part of her that he was sidetracking had nothing to do with forest fires, so she did her best to ignore that and left him in place.

He clearly had no experience with wildfire or hotshot techniques, but show him something once and he had it solid.

Not just what to do, but like he'd always had it. Luke had clearly never run a chainsaw, didn't even know how to start one. Yet after a single day that the team had spent clearing some new land for a farmer downslope near the town of Monitor, he moved like a three-year sawyer.

And he never spoke much. Strong and silent type. "Just takin' care of business, ma'am" attitude. When he did speak, his voice had a soft southern to it, Tennessee or Kentucky—that he clearly knew was a total charmer. Of the six women among the recruits, four had already taken a run at him. As far as Candace could tell, not a one of them had gotten past that polite shield.

What are you hiding, Rawlings?

He wasn't saying. Well, today should separate out more of the recruits. Question was, did she want him separated out or not?

She moved them downslope from where they'd camped—an uncomfortable site on the slopes of Dragontail Peak. Anyone who thought fires didn't burn on this kind of terrain, so hotshots never walked it, would be disabused of that notion over the fast-approaching fire season.

When they reached a small clearing, her dad had already arrived with a wildfire engine. These trucks were wide, heavy, and smaller than the standard in-town engines. More the size of a utility service truck, they could cross surprisingly rough terrain with a great deal of gear and five hundred gallons of water.

Once they were gathered, Candace pulled out a fire shelter pouch and held it up for all to see.

"This is a five-hundred dollar device of last resort. You will always have one on your hip and you will protect it more carefully than your own face. If everything else goes wrong and you find yourself in a burnover situation, this foil shelter is your only chance of survival."

That sobered a number of their faces.

"Today, we'll practice with plastic shelters worth about ten dollars. I don't want to see even the smallest tear or nick in these, because if it's a real fire, fifteen hundred degree flame will find its way right through that gap and toast your ass. I can't begin to tell you how much paperwork that will cause me."

That got her some good laughs. Even the old hands appreciated the dark humor of it. She knew that at least three of them besides herself had ridden out a burnover under a shelter. And several of them had friends among the Yarnell 19 who died in 2013; the manzanita-fed flames too hot for even the foil shelters' protection.

Luke Rawlings, however, looked at her as if she'd just committed a crime against humanity. His expression had gone dark enough that she suddenly feared for her safety. No. It wasn't her he was looking at. He was looking at something that wasn't in the grass clearing, but rather in his past. Well, she pitied whoever had put that look on his face, because she'd wager they hadn't survived long after whatever they'd done to piss him off.

She made it a policy to not pull a recruit's application file during the ten-day trial, but she'd broken down last night. U.S. Navy Chief Petty Officer Luke Rawlings, retired. That explained some things, but not others. She'd fought fire beside plenty of ex-soldiers before, though none as quietly competent as Rawlings. Many hadn't been able to face the fire itself when it came down to reality: some froze, some ran, and one got the shakes so bad they had to medevac him out.

Luke was steady. Always helping the rawest rookies get their feet under them with a gentle word and a clear demonstration. Infinitely patient, he kept working with them until they really had it. He'd be a good man to have around.

Erase that, Cantrell.

Mr. Ex-Navy Luke Altman would be a good *firefighter* to have around. She just wished she could stop thinking about the *man* who watched her as much as she was watching him.

Usually about half of the former soldiers would be weeded out by the fire shelter deployment exercise.

It was something of a surprise when she realized that she really hoped Luke wasn't one of those.

4

Deep breathing barely pulled Luke back from the edge.

Pine scent.

Not jungle.

Dry air.

Better.

He'd been civilian for six months now, and no day was easier.

The only easy day was yesterday!

He kept repeating the SEAL motto to himself, but it wasn't helping. "Yesterday" had totally sucked as well.

There was no way to predict when it was going to slap him; half his team gone between one breath and the next. They'd been deep in the Democratic Republic of the Congo having a quiet moment in a quiet town. The woman had strolled by where they were eating lunch with a basket of melons balanced on her head. The brightly-colored flowing *kanga* had hidden only parts of her fine form; the part that had been five kilos of explosives. The blast had ripped her, half his team, and one whole end of a Congolese market to shreds.

He did his best to focus on Candace Cantrell's lecture about how to deploy a fire shelter.

Breathe in the dry pine.

Piece by piece he forced his brain back together.

Only easy day was yesterday.

U.S. soil, not the Congo.

Training here—way easier than any single day of BUD/S.

Essential survival techniques that didn't include flak vests and Kevlar helmets. Weapons of the forest were a Pulaski tool and a chainsaw, not an M-249 SAW machine gun and Barrett M107 sniper rifle.

Luke dug the toe of his boot into the thick mountain bunch grass, appreciating Candace's steady manner and calm voice. Getting easily lost in it. She'd been growing more and more crucial to his daily control, his well being.

Anyone who'd served and said that each day wasn't a massive struggle was only lying to himself. But being around Candace made that struggle seem worthwhile.

That thought finally kicked him all the way out of his downloop and left him blinking at her in surprise.

She was important to him.

How the hell had that happened?

Women were…

Not like her. It's like she was a different breed or species or something. A better one.

Some part of his brain, trained by far too many officer harangues, had kept up with the lecture. She now stood close enough that he could smell her—like sweet honey and glacier-fed streams—as she had him stepping into the shelter, pulling it up over his back and his head, and lying down with his face in a hole dug into the dirt.

"Keep your face in the hole, it's where the air is coolest," Candace called out loud enough to be heard easily through the shelter. "Feet to the fire. Your team leader may call out a last moment shift. If so, you keep your face in the hole and rotate your feet around. Do not, I repeat, do not lift the edge of your shelter. That is a life-and-death decision. The edges stay down even when you think you'll go mad."

Great! Just what Luke needed, another reason to lose it.

"Fire is loud. Freight train loud. It will try to rip away your shelter. Don't let it."

And then all hell broke loose.

His shelter slapped down on him!

A thunderclap of noise!

He was back in battle! God, no!

He fought the urge to scream.

Struggled for focus.

Orders.

His commander had said to hold fast. To stay down. Under cover. He gripped the edges of his shelter harder than he'd clutched the stock of his MP5N machine pistol as he was blown backward into a goat merchant's stall. Gripped so hard he wondered that his fingers didn't break.

He heard a voice yelling out, "Stay under the shelter!"

The blast moved away, battered another shelter nearby, returned! and then moved off again. It was…the spray of a fire hose off the wildfire engine. Water began to trickle under the edge of the shelter.

Shit.

Not a bomb.

Not a war.

He racked in a painful breath. Just a test with water. No cracked ribs this time, he could breathe. He started laughing…then crying. Mickey, Ralph, Doug; shooting the shit over Ndakala fish curry one second and scattered in pieces the next.

Water flowed under the edge of the shelter and he couldn't stop it.

Couldn't stop it as it flowed out of his eyes as well.

For the first time in the year since he'd lost them, he wept into his dirt hole in the ground as the cleansing water washed over and under him inside the safety of his little shelter.

A woman's voice kept calling to him that it would all be okay, just stay safe.

5

Candace sat at the edge of the grass clearing, outside the circle of firelight, and watched the final twenty sitting around the campfire. Day Ten, they'd made it. And just as importantly, so had she. The Leavenworth IHC was happening.

Dad and the department's mostly volunteer crew had delivered hotdogs and burgers with all the trimmings, massive bags of chips, and local craft beer. The whole team's laughter had that easy confidence of a crew who'd formed up well.

She really had done it. Another three weeks of serious training and she'd list the team as ready for call out. They'd done a carefully controlled prescribed burn on Day Eight and not a one of them had flinched, which boded well. The only test left was one she couldn't arrange, facing an angry wildfire on the run. That final trial she'd have to leave up to the whim of Mother Nature and the needs of the U.S. Forest Service.

"Thinking pretty hard there, Cantrell." Luke handed her a fresh beer then waved his own at the spot beside her, asking permission before he sat on the grass.

"I do that sometimes," she nodded for him to join her. He did, stretching out his legs and leaning back on his elbows, but not too close. That southern gentleman thing that made him such a standout from normal guys.

Having sought her out, he remained silent.

"Something shifted for you during the training. Something big." When he'd gone under the shelter, she'd thought she was going to lose him for sure, but when he'd emerged…

His shrug was noncommittal. Guy-speak for *maybe*.

"All your pieces fit."

"Say what?" That got his attention away from the team around the campfire to studying her closely out here in the shadows.

"When you first showed up, it's like you were fractured. All made up of different pieces that didn't really fit together. That's gone now."

Again that long quiet study. She didn't turn to face him.

Couldn't.

A team was just that, especially when you were the leader. By season's end, these people would be as close as brothers and sisters—to her, to each other. But Luke Rawlings made her wish for different things. Things she'd rather he didn't see.

"Pretty forthright there."

His accusation was accurate so she didn't waste time denying it.

He turned to watch the fire once more.

She hoped she hadn't scared him off. Though he didn't look like a man who scared easily.

"You remind me of my last commander. Lieutenant Commander Altman was about as straight ahead as they come."

"Is that a compliment?"

"You have no idea, lady. Compliments don't come any higher. And SEAL commanders don't come any better than Altman."

"You're a SEAL?" she finally turned to look at him and discovered his dark eyes studying her from close by.

"Past tense."

"No wonder you're so damn good at everything. Besides, is there such a thing as a past tense SEAL?"

He grimaced, "Not really."

She'd never met— "I've never met anyone like you. You just seem so—" safe.

A job didn't get much less safe than leading an Interagency Hotshot Crew, no matter that safety was their number one priority.

"—so…Shit!" Words were failing her beneath his dark gaze.

"Never met a woman like you either 'Not Candy' Cantrell." His deep voice was a little rough. "Can't seem to stop thinking about you. Even invading my damned dreams." He looked disgusted.

"Wet ones, Mr. SEAL?"

His easy laugh wrapped around them both acknowledging the pun and the way she'd learned to deal with that line head on.

"White dress ones, lady."

Candace could feel herself freezing up. Yet another man who thought she belonged in some neat bride-wifely pigeon-hole. So not her.

"White dress made of Nomex," Luke mused half to himself. "How's that for an amazing image?"

Nomex was the material used in making fire gear, became a second skin to a hotshot.

Luke dreamed of her as a firefighter? Every man she'd ever been with had tried to talk her out of it. To him, or at least his subconscious, it was an integral part of her. Something no one else except her father had ever understood.

She'd never been a big one on dreams, never remembered the ones at night, or made up ones during the day. But she couldn't deny that she'd had her eye, and her thoughts, on Luke Altman since the day he'd stepped off his big Harley and joined the hotshot trials.

She could feel him watching her by the warm shadows of firelight. Quiet like a SEAL and patient like a gentleman. Strong enough to sweep her away and safe enough that she'd never think he'd do something without permission.

Turning to study him, she did her best to look inside herself, never one of her strengths.

Did she want to grant that permission?

Big time.

Well, he'd called you forthright as a compliment, so what are you waiting on?

Nothing.

Candace leaned down to kiss him.

After an initial grunt of surprise, he proved that cutting down trees and digging soil weren't the only things he was exceptionally skilled at. She melted against his heat until they both groaned together.

She could feel their smiles start in that instant and continue to grow. When it threatened to turn into laughter of sheer joy, she moved back until she too was resting against the soft grasses on her elbows and facing the campfire and the celebrating crews.

So, her heart wanted to race as fast as his Harley? She'd let it.

"Going to be an interesting summer, Mr. Hotshot," Candace did her best to keep her tone casual as the heat continued to ripple deliciously through her body.

"I'm thinking it could be a whole lot more than one of them..." he paused long enough for her to turn and see his smile,

"…Sweet Candy Fire."

Candace turned back to the fire, but could feel her smile going goofy.

She was thinking exactly the same thing.

About the Author

M. L. Buchman has over 30 novels in print. His military romantic suspense books have been named Barnes & Noble and NPR "Top 5 of the year" and Booklist "Top 10 of the Year." In addition to romance, he also writes thrillers, fantasy, and science fiction.

In among his career as a corporate project manager he has: rebuilt and single-handed a fifty-foot sailboat, both flown and jumped out of airplanes, designed and built two houses, and bicycled solo around the world. He is now making his living as a full-time writer on the Oregon Coast with his beloved wife. He is constantly amazed at what you can do with a degree in Geophysics. You may keep up with his writing by subscribing to his newsletter at *www.mlbuchman.com.*

Full Blaze
a Firehawks romance

Cal Jackson stared up at the wall of flame
eating its way toward him through the forest.
He was always tempting fate one step too
far. Now he was way past the second step,
as well as the third. He was standing in
the foreign land of totally screwed. In his

seven years of fighting wildfires and five more photographing them, he'd never been this far over the line. Not even close.

He'd ridden the edge a lot since he was a testosterone-laden teen. It had earned him his fair share of cold slaps from ticked-off women, but maybe more than his share of warm and friendly nights. It had also led to numerous interesting opportunities to travel for both work and play, so he'd learned to take that risk without really thinking about it.

He tried not to take that second step very often; it was his warning that he was pushing the limits. But dancing along the edge of that step was what had won him so many of his awards. Though the Pulitzer for photography and "best of" for World Press Photo still remained out of reach, he'd bagged a lot of awards including the cover on *National Geographic*. And *Time*, twice.

Out here, way past the second step, the Grindstone Canyon Fire was in full-throated roar. The sound throbbed against his body with bass notes that actually shook his inner organs. He'd stood close beside the tracks when two-hundred-car freight trains had flown past at full speed. This was louder. Nor did it conveniently pass by and Doppler into the distance; this train of fire had him clear in its sights.

The air was growing so hot that it hurt to breathe. His acute sense of smell for smoke, burning pitch, and carbon had long since been overwhelmed by the saturation of them in the air. He'd embedded tight with a crew of hotshot firefighters who were fast losing ground against the wildfire despite their best efforts. It happened that way. Fighting fire was a delicate back-and-forth dance between flame and attacker, almost like a hip-hop advance and retreat, attack and counterattack by both sides of the…hoedown.

Hoedown? Where had he come up with that? Third foster father.

Yuck!

In one way the comparison was appropriate, as it was with the rakes, Pulaskis, and even hoes that a hotshot crew used to battle the flames. Not hoedown, but rather… His brain trying to work out what hip-hop dancers called that battle of dance, power, and sensuality had to be about the damn stupidest thought to have as his last on earth.

The Grindstone in southern California was probably the last big fire of the year in the United States. The Pacific Northwest was already getting rain, and Colorado had snow, though that hadn't slowed down the Fern Lake Fire back in 2012. He'd won two awards and gotten national headlines on that one for his piece on fighting wildfires when the supply tanks and rivers froze and the helicopters couldn't get at the water to fight the flames.

The Southeast had just been soaked by a really serious trio of hurricanes. So this year California was last in the hot seat, and the fires above Santa Barbara were doing their best to take back the hills for Mother Nature. It had started in the same area of Rattlesnake Canyon Park as the lethal Rattlesnake Fire of 1953 that killed fifteen firefighters. Though this time it was started by lightning rather than a psycho arsonist.

You'd think he'd have grabbed a clue from the historical setting, though he'd been no better with history than most of the subjects in school, except fighting and photography. With maturity, he'd added "fire" as an adjective to both of them. He now knew fire history as well as any hotshot walking the hills, except for this time when it should have warned him. There hadn't been a bad burn here in more than sixty years, so it was due.

The hotshot crew he'd been with had been in the heat for a week, driving ahead and then retreating—dancing that careful strategic dance against the fire. Less than two minutes ago the crew had taken off down a narrow track leading across a cliff face and onto a rolling slope that led down into the distant valley. Their escape route was clean. He'd hesitated an extra fifteen seconds to get a shot of a massive fig tree, over eighty feet tall, being ripped up by fire-generated winds and tossed aside like a matchstick. Fifteen lousy seconds.

The problem was that the fire had cast the flaming tree down right across his escape route. The tree not only lay across the path, but was catching all of the surrounding material on fire as well. The crew looked at him helplessly across the gap.

The notch canyon that separated them was too far for a rope cast, and the vertical walls that plunged down to either side of his position required a level of mountaineering skill that included hammers and pitons, neither of which he was carrying. He carefully eyed a ledge about ten feet below, but could think of no way to get down to it. Far too narrow a landing to risk a jump. Yet.

He could see the crew boss on the radio, but with the fire's roar, Cal couldn't hear him even though his own radio handset was in its pouch right against his shoulder and the volume was turned up to full.

The smoke blotted out the boss just as he was about to make a hand sign of some sort. A glance upward into the smoke canopy told him that no helicopters would be able to save his sorry behind. The mushroom cloud of smoke—looking like a nuclear blast it was so intense—rose ten thousand feet above the California landscape would block any line of approach.

The ravine to the south was clogged with fire, and the one to the north was now fully lit by the thrown tree, its branches ablaze like a thousand-armed candelabra. The two ravines met to the west. The only way out was east—and there raged the beast.

The narrow ledge of his final demise was covered in a few dogwood and valley oak trees, tall grasses, and dense manzanita brush. When the fire rolled over this site, it would burn hot. Hot in the same way it

had burned over the nineteen-man crew
at Yarnell, the air so superheated it had
burned right through their foil emergency
shelters. It had done that despite the cir-
cular clearing they'd cut around themselves.
And he didn't even carry a chain saw to
try to make a clearing. All he had were his
cameras.

He backed to the edge of the precipice
and then turned once more to look at the
flame. He wasn't even conscious of his
actions as he lifted his new Canon Mark III
camera, found the frame, shot the photo.
Zoomed back. Found the next, shot it. The
beast was close. He'd only once been so
close to the heart of the firestorm. During
his days as a member of a hotshot crew,
they'd have been long gone before the heart
of the fire rolled this close. The camera was
actually heating in his hands, prickly hot to
hold.

Too close! That was it. He dropped
the camera into his bag and pulled out his
old workhorse 6D body with the 28 mm

wide-angle lens. No way he'd risk a lens change with all of the dust and ash in the air.

There! He could see the image coming together that would make a cover photo. Another prize-winner was almost here. Just a few more seconds… If he could just…

A metal shape zipped by the lens, fast. He didn't see what it was, but some instinct had him pressing the shutter. He flicked back to the image.

On his viewfinder a winged drone a half-dozen feet in length, painted black with gold-and-orange flames, had flown between him and the fire. It had a bold "MHA" emblazoned on its side.

Some comfort that was. All it meant was that someone from Mount Hood Aviation was going to have the award-winning photo of the journalist who burned alive while clutching his camera like a damned idiot. All because he'd had to take that third step and now couldn't wrench back from it.

Cal was going to make a lousy Cinderella, no pretty gown rising from the ashes for him. But he was sure going to end up as a cinder. Another thirty seconds and he'd have to take his chances inside the foil shelter, though he'd sworn he'd never do that again.

Maybe his life was supposed to pass before his eyes right about now, but he hoped not. He'd beaten the first sixteen years of his life down with every ounce of a firefighter's willpower until they didn't exist. The time since had been mostly good, but with the way his luck was running today, he'd get to see those early days before he'd named himself Calvin Jackson.

Some idiot part of him started to raise the camera again, but then he stopped. His cameras were going to cook right along with him, even if he threw himself over them like a Marine covering a grenade to save his buddies. For once he just looked at the wall of flame. Its heart so hot it glowed gold as the fire swarmed up tree trunks six stories tall with a single breath, sheathing each tree in a cloak of flame just six inches and fifteen hundred degrees thick. The roar deepened as if gathering its breath. So loud that—

The sharp blast of a voice over a loudspeaker not ten feet behind him so startled Cal that he almost stumbled off the ledge. Completely masked by the roar of the fire and with hundred-foot flames less than thirty yards away, a helicopter had come to hover behind him. It wore the same paint job as the drone.

A glance up showed the rotor blades shimmering in a lethal arc just a few feet above him and no break in the smoke-cloud cover above. The hotshot crew was still invisible across the ravine. But far down below, right off the narrow spit of cliff he was perched upon, he could see the terrain. The pilot had flown up through a hole underneath the smoke and ash cloud.

"Get aboard, you bloody git!" the speaker screamed at him. He wouldn't have heard it if it weren't less than ten feet away and aimed right at him.

The chopper hung just out of reach, hovering with its open side door toward him. Over his shoulder he could see that the spinning rotor disk was within a foot or so of a stout oak tree. They couldn't fly any closer to him. The chopper didn't even have skids to grab on to like they always did in the movies, just wheels.

The cargo bay door was an open four-by-four-foot square of salvation, hanging a half-dozen feet away over a hundred-yard drop. He stuffed both cameras into the padded bag, snapped it shut, and chucked the bag through the door toward the rear so it wouldn't go out the other side, which was also open. Then, squatting to make the leap while the chopper bounced in the roiling air currents, he jumped into space.

He landed mostly inside the door. Far enough to drag himself the rest of the way. He spotted a rope line, made sure it was secured to something, then snapped the D ring on the front of his safety harness onto it so that he was now secure.

"Good to go," he shouted to the pilot. There was no way he could be heard. The freight train was screaming toward them, barely ten yards from the rotor tips.

The pilot, flying alone, risked a quick glance back, but was skilled enough for the chopper to remain rock stable despite the turbulent environment.

Cal only had long enough to get the impression of a narrow face and mirrored shades wrapped in a large, earmuff pilot's headset. Seeing he was aboard, the pilot rolled the chopper hard left and dove down through the dwindling smoke hole. He caught the camera bag as it skidded across the deck plating.

A glance up at the cliff showed a tongue of flame now reaching out to grab where the chopper had hovered only moments before.

Now that he was safe, the adrenal rush kicked out hard. He'd fought fires from California to Alaska, and he'd photographed them in Brazil, Russia, and a dozen other places. He'd never before had his hands shake so badly that he couldn't even open the bag to make sure the cameras were okay. All he could do was clench it to his chest and let the shakes run through him.

***

"Yeah, Ground Command. This is Hawk Oh-two, I got him. You can release your crew to the next site."

Jeannie Clark clicked off her mike and the one-word acknowledgment came right back. She was bummed. She'd finally found a flaw with her beautiful new Firehawk. Well, almost new. The machine had done a couple tours in Iraq first, but it had been totally renovated, repainted, and reconfigured with a big belly tank for dumping retardant on wildfires. It was new to her. Her boss and MHA's lead pilot, Emily Beale, had only just certified her in this type last month. And the chopper was also new to Mount Hood Aviation's "Hoodies," one of the country's premier firefighters-for-hire contractors. It was only the second load-rated Type I helicopter in their inventory.

Until recently, she'd only been certified in the midsize Type II Twin Huey 212 and the tiny Type III MD500, both much-lower-capacity crafts. The Firehawk was built on the Sikorsky Black Hawk frame and could lift a massive thousand gallons of retardant or water, about four and a half tons. That could make a serious dent in a blaze except when Mama Nature was really kicking up her heels with Papa Fire. That was what her Australian friend Dale always called them, as if they were part of his Aboriginal Dreamtime creation mysticism. She'd looked up the expression and it wasn't, but she'd kept using it even after coming to America. People always looked at her cross-eyed when she used it, so she now kept it to herself.

The thing was, with her MD500, she could have scooted right onto that cliff edge instead of hovering out in space.

Had to give the guy some points—at three hundred feet up a cliff, he'd jumped right out with no hesitation. That said something about guts, or desperation. She'd half expected him to freeze and die there. Even three more seconds and she'd have had to bug out and leave him there to burn.

Available at fine retailers every-where December, 2014

More information at:
www.mlbuchman.com